In the year 776 BC, the first
Olympic Games were held in a town
called Olympia in Ancient Greece.
Many years later, a boy named Olly
grew up there, dreaming of being
an Olympic champion. But first,
he would have to be better than his
arch-enemy, Spiro...

ORCHARD BOOKS
338 Euston Road, London NW1 3BH
Orchard Books Australia
Level 17/207 Kent Street, Sydney, NSW 2000

First published in 2011
First paperback publication in 2012

ISBN 978 1 40831 179 0 (hardback)
ISBN 978 1 40831 187 5 (paperback)

A CIP catalogue record for this book is available
from the British Library.

1 3 5 7 9 10 8 6 4 2 (hardback)
1 3 5 7 9 10 8 6 4 2 (paperback)

Printed in Great Britain

Orchard Books is a division of Hachette Children's Books,
an Hachette UK company.

www.hachette.co.uk

OLYMPIA

RUN LIKE THE WIND

SHOO RAYNER

ORCHARD

CHAPTER ONE

"There's only one way you'll ever run faster than me!" growled Spiro.

"Oh yeah?" Olly challenged his arch-enemy. He put his hands on his hips and stood his ground. "How?"

Spiro sneered. "I'll show you." He called to his dog and pointed at Olly. "Kill him, Kerberos!" he growled.

"Wooah!" Olly took off like a shot.

Spiro's snarling dog lunged towards Olly with sharp, vicious teeth bared in foaming jaws. His wild, staring eyes rolled in deep, dark sockets.

"E-e-e-yow!" Olly yelled, leaping into the air as he heard the dog's teeth snap together behind him. "Run faster! Faster!" Olly told himself.

"Ha, ha!" Spiro yelled after him. "You'll never beat *me* in the Boys' Athletics Festival."

"I'll beat you one day!" Olly shouted defiantly. "Just you wait and…*yow*!"

Gritting his teeth, Olly ran for his life. If Kerberos caught up with him, he wouldn't be able to sit down for weeks, let alone win a running race!

"It's so unfair," Olly complained to himself, as he ran helter-skelter through the streets of Olympia. "I was so close to beating Spiro in training today. I shouldn't even have to race against him – he's a year older than me!"

Olly pumped his arms and picked up his feet. As he weaved in and out of the shoppers in the busy marketplace, Kerberos yapped and growled behind him.

Up ahead, Olly saw the statue
of Leonidas of Rhodes, the greatest
runner the Olympic Games had
ever known.

"Help me, Leonidas!" he called up
to the statue.

"He can't hear you!" someone in
the crowd joked.

"Oh, great, they're
laughing at me!" Olly
grumbled. "This is
so embarrassing!"

Olly was exhausted. Every time Kerberos tried to take a bite out of him, Olly had to leap away from his snapping jaws! Only fear kept him going.

"I'll slip down behind the Temple of Hermes," Olly told himself. "That might confuse the evil monster."

It was a good idea – but not good enough. Kerberos seemed to sense Olly's plan. The dog ran up the temple steps and charged through the smouldering remains of a burnt sacrifice, scattering smoke and cinders everywhere. Now he was right above Olly.

The crazy animal leaped from the wall, opened his mouth wide and aimed his teeth at Olly's backside.

Olly closed his eyes and waited for the pain...

"Kerberos! BEHAVE YOURSELF!" a girl's voice called firmly through the smoky air.

Kerberos crashed to the ground behind Olly. He rolled over a couple of times, tucked his tail between his legs and trotted back up the temple steps like a gentle lapdog.

As the smoke cleared, Olly saw his sister, Chloe, and her best friend, Hebe, petting Kerberos. Chloe was scratching his tummy! The dog's tongue lolled from the side of his mouth and his back leg twitched with joy.

"Chloe! Hebe!" Olly panted. "I'm so glad you were there. Spiro set Kerberos on me. I thought I was going to be dog meat!"

"You wouldn't eat Olly, would you, boy?" Chloe cooed at Kerberos.

Kerberos turned his dark patch eye towards Olly and winked. He was Spiro's dog, but it was Chloe he really loved. He was putty in her hands.

"That Spiro doesn't deserve to have Kerberos!" Chloe sighed. "Does he, Kerby-werby?"

"If I'm going to win the Olympic Games when I grow up," Olly explained to Chloe, "I have to start by beating Spiro and winning the race in the Boys' Athletics Festival."

Chloe and Olly's dad, Ariston, ran the gymnasium where all the great athletes trained for the Olympic Games that were held in Olympia every four years.

Olly and Spiro both worked at the gym, helping with odd jobs. They also picked up skills by watching the athletes, who used to train and compete naked!

Every boy in Olympia dreamed of winning a race at the Boys' Festival. It was the first step on the way to becoming an Olympic champion.

But the Boys' Athletics Festival was only two days away. Olly knew he needed help to make him run faster, and he needed it *now*.

The great statue of Hermes, god of athletics, glared at Olly from a pedestal high above the temple door. The golden feathers on his winged cap and winged sandals glinted in the bright sunlight.

"If I had Hermes' winged sandals," Olly declared, "I could beat anyone. I could run like the wind!"

CHAPTER TWO

Chloe turned to her best friend, Hebe.
"I bet your dad could ask Hermes
to help Olly. He *is* the Temple Priest,
after all."

"Hmmm…" Hebe mused.
"I suppose there's no harm in asking.
Let's go and try."

Olly had never
been inside the
temple before.
"Are you
sure we're
allowed in?"
he asked
nervously.

"Of course we are!" Hebe giggled. She took his arm and dragged him through the archway into the murky darkness of the inner temple.

Hebe's dad was kneeling in front of an altar, chanting hymns.

"Dad," Hebe whispered. "Olly needs to run like the wind so he can beat that horrible Spiro in the Boys' Athletics Festival. Do you think Hermes can help?"

Hebe's dad stroked his beard and studied Olly closely. In a low, gravelly voice he said, "Bring me two small birds." Then he turned away and began chanting again.

"Why does he want two birds?" Olly asked, blinking as they emerged in the bright sunshine outside.

"Don't ask why," Hebe said mysteriously. "Just do it!"

I could buy a pair of birds in the market, Olly thought to himself. *But I don't have any money, and besides, Hermes might think that's cheating. I'll have to catch them myself.*

While Chloe and Hebe took Kerberos back to Spiro, Olly looked for a basket and a length of string.

In a quiet olive grove, Olly set up his trap. He placed a basket upside down on the ground, and held up the front edge with a twig.

He put a handful of stale bread under the basket, tied a length of string to the twig and trailed it to his hiding place in a nearby bush.

It wasn't long before sparrows spotted the grain and edged towards the trap.

"Gotcha!" Olly cheered as he pulled the string.

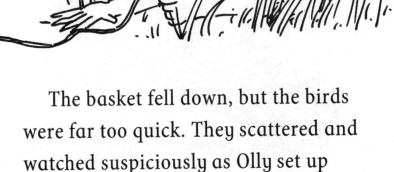

The basket fell down, but the birds were far too quick. They scattered and watched suspiciously as Olly set up the trap again.

He had to wait a long time
before the birds decided it was safe.
Eventually a couple of birds began
feeding under the basket.

"*Wait for it…wait for it!*" Olly
whispered to himself. "*Ready…
steady…now!*" Olly yanked the string
and the basket crashed down over the
poor unsuspecting birds.

"Woohoo! Two
sparrows!" he
cheered. "Just
what I needed."
Olly gently
tied up the
basket and
headed off
towards the
temple.

Hebe's dad smiled when Olly presented his catch.

"It took me ages to trap them," Olly said. "Do you think Hermes will be pleased?"

"Come back tomorrow," Hebe's dad said in his slow, gruff voice. "Hermes will have something for you then."

Olly could hardly sleep that night. His mind raced as he gazed at the twinkling stars through his window.

"How will the sacrifice of two small birds help Hermes make me run like the wind?" he wondered.

CHAPTER THREE

The next morning, Olly made his way to the temple, to see if Hermes had anything for him.

"I'm sure Hermes wants me to beat Spiro," Olly told himself. "Who would want to be on Spiro's side?"

Hebe and her dad were waiting for Olly. Hebe walked solemnly down the temple steps and presented him with a folded linen cloth.

Wrapped inside were two tiny pairs of wings. Each pair was tied onto a strip of soft leather.

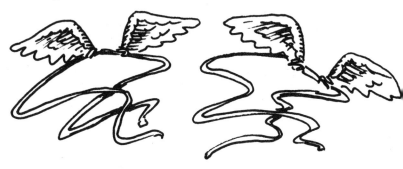

Hebe's dad smiled wisely. "These wings are gifts from Hermes," he explained. "Tie them to your ankles when you race and believe that you can win!" His eyes twinkled in the early morning sun.

"Thank you!" exclaimed Olly.

Olly spent the rest of the day keeping out of Spiro's way. There was plenty to do at the gym, like collecting javelins...

...and discuses...

...and returning them for the athletes to throw again.

At mealtime, Olly and Spiro laid out the tables in the dining hall with a loaf of flat bread for each athlete…

…bowls of cheese…

…and olives and salad.

After washing and dressing, the athletes filed in and gave thanks to the gods for their food. They ate in silence while Simonedes, the history teacher, told them stories about the gods.

Simonedes was old and wrinkled like a walnut, but his powerful voice was as clear as a bell.

He explained how mighty Zeus, the greatest god of all, made Hermes his messenger.

"Zeus gave Hermes winged sandals that let him speed across the world faster than the wind," Simonedes explained. "That's why Hermes is the god of athletics and why he looks after all great athletes."

The athletes raised their cups in the air and called out with one voice, "Hermes! Let us run like the wind and win all our races!"

"*Let us run like the wind and win all our races!*" Olly repeated under his breath. He felt for the linen cloth that was tucked into his belt. He had his own wings from Hermes now.

The walls of the dining room were painted with pictures of Hermes flying across the heavens. Olly gazed at them and imagined himself racing across the clouds too...

A sharp smack on the head soon brought him back to earth.

"Oi! Daydreamer!" Spiro jeered. "You ready for the last training session before the Boys' Athletics Festival?"

Olly blinked and looked around him. The athletes had finished their meal. He began clearing the tables with a knowing smile on his face. "I'm going to beat you today, Spiro!" Olly said quietly.

Spiro was bigger, stronger and meaner than Olly. He leaned over him and stared menacingly into his eyes. "See you at the starting line, slowcoach!" he sneered.

Olly touched the linen cloth again to reassure himself. But he said nothing. He just smiled and got on with his work.

A shadow passed over Spiro's face. He wanted Olly to be scared of him!

CHAPTER FOUR

The boys had been allowed to train on the sacred running track of Olympia. It let them feel what it would be like to compete as grown-ups and it sharpened their racing skills.

Olly walked down the dark tunnel that led to the stadium. *I will walk this way the day I become an Olympic champion!* he thought.

All the boys who were competing in the Boys' Athletics Festival had come to the final training session.

Olly's dad, Ariston, called them to the starting line for their last practice race.

Olly quickly tied the wings to his ankles. They made him feel light and bouncy. Then Olly placed his toes in the grooves cut into the marble slabs that stretched across the starting line.

Spiro spotted Olly's wings and laughed. "Ha! Are you going to fly, little birdy?"

"We'll see," Olly whispered to himself. He crouched down and focused on the finish line in the distance. "Hermes," he muttered under his breath, "let me honour your faith in me by beating Spiro and winning the race today."

"*Go!*" yelled Ariston.

Olly sprang forward like a gazelle. All he could think of was winning. He felt as though he was flying. Everything was perfect – his breathing, his pace and his legs, which seemed to stretch out further than they had ever done before.

Olly could hear Spiro grunting beside him. They were neck and neck…

The finish line came upon Olly in a blur. He wasn't sure who had won!

"It's a draw!" called Ariston. "Olly and Spiro came joint first!"

Olly threw his hands in the air. "I'm a winner!" he cheered.

"Cheat!" Spiro panted. He pushed Olly to the ground and tore the wings from his ankles. He crushed them and threw them in the dirt.

"Those wings are magic and magic is cheating!" Spiro spat, and stalked off towards the changing rooms.

Later, Olly explained everything to his dad. Ariston sighed and said, "Well, I'm afraid Spiro's right. You can't wear the wings at the festival."

Olly stared at the sad, crumpled feathers. "They won't work now, anyway," he sniffed.

Ariston touched his son's head. He knew how much Olly wanted to beat Spiro and win the race.

"Hermes has shown you that you are *as fast as* Spiro," he explained. "Only you can prove that you are *faster.*"

CHAPTER FIVE

"I hate him!" Olly cursed, angrily throwing the broken wings onto the dusty ground outside the gym.

Chloe sighed and picked them up. She'd been putting up with the battle between Olly and Spiro for years. Spiro knew all the little ways to make Olly lose his temper.

"That's no way to treat a gift from Hermes," she said.

"Fat lot of good it did me!" Olly grumbled. "I'll never beat Spiro now."

"Let's go and see Hebe's dad," Chloe soothed. "I'm sure he'll know what to do."

𐄷𐄷𐄷𐄷𐄷𐄷𐄷

"You tied with Spiro?" Hebe's dad smiled. "Well, that is marvellous!"

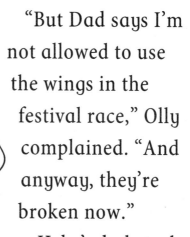

"But Dad says I'm not allowed to use the wings in the festival race," Olly complained. "And anyway, they're broken now."

Hebe's dad stroked his beard while he thought about what to do.

"You don't need the wings any more," he said. "*You* ran as fast as Spiro, not the wings. Hermes was with you and he will always be with you. You just have to *believe* you can do it and run faster than you've ever run before."

He led Olly and Chloe up some steps to the smoking embers of the sacrificial altar.

"Give your wings back to Hermes. Prove that you have faith in yourself. Hermes will find a way to guide you to victory."

Olly stared at the little wings. Could he still beat Spiro and win the race without them?

Chloe nodded and motioned to him to do as he was told. She knew what was best for him better than anyone.

Olly felt a surge of determination flood through him. He tossed the little wings onto the fire. The feathers flared in a burst of flame.

As the thick smoke spiralled towards the heavens, Olly whispered a little prayer: "Hermes, I will not fail your faith in me."

CHAPTER SIX

The whole town turned out to watch the festival. The competitors were still just boys, but one day the people of Olympia hoped they would grow up to be their Olympic champions.

Hundreds of people sat on the grassy banks of the stadium. As they ate their picnics, the sense of excitement and expectation grew.

Olly's stomach fluttered as he made his way to the starting line of the running race.

"Lost your wings, little birdy?" Spiro jeered.

"Don't listen to him," Olly told himself. "This is it. You can beat him. You CAN win!"

Olly placed his toes in the starting grooves and thought about what Hebe's dad had told him. Olly knew he had to believe in himself.

The runners were kept in line behind a taught rope called the *hysplex*. When it was triggered, the rope would snap down to the ground as the signal to start the race.

The *hysplex* was used for the professional athletes' races and Olly had never started with it before.

"Don't trip on the rope!" Olly told himself again and again.

The starter announced that the boys were ready and the crowd hushed.

Olly stared at the finish line in the distance. Now his only thought was to run like the wind!

"*Go!*" The *hysplex* rope snapped to the ground. A line of dust puffed into the air. Olly leaped out of the starting grooves and flew cleanly over the rope. The race was on!

The crowd leaped to their feet with a roar of cheering. But all Olly could hear was the rush of blood in his ears, and the pounding of his heart and feet as he tore down the sacred race track.

Spiro wasn't going to let Olly win easily. He put everything he had into the race. They were neck and neck again, in front of everyone else. The other boys in the race were already just a memory.

The adult athletes were all in the crowd and they cheered from the side: "Come on Olly! You can do it!"

Just then, Spiro coughed loudly and spat. A huge sticky gob flew through the air and landed on Olly's face.

"Eurrgh!" As Olly wiped his face with his arm, he lost his balance and stumbled…

Olly lurched and jerked along the
track for three or four paces. He was
determined not to fall over, but by the
time he had recovered, Spiro was well
in the lead.

They were over halfway down
the course by now. Olly would never
make up the lost ground.

"Ha, ha!" Spiro snarled, as he raced towards the finish line. "I'm going to win again!"

Just then, out of the corner of his eye, Olly noticed Chloe. She was crouched at the side of the track, trying to keep Kerberos under control.

The noise of the crowd was driving Kerberos wild. He was too strong for Chloe! He slipped out of her grasp and shot onto the course like a beast possessed. Hungry for blood, the dog's mad, red eyes were firmly fixed on Olly's backside again!

Fear gripped Olly and twisted his insides. "Hermes! Save me!" he screamed.

Olly felt a surge of power and determination flood through him. As if someone had pulled the levers of a *hysplex* inside him, Olly leaped forward as his legs pumped even faster than before.

Olly was shoulder to shoulder with Spiro now! His enemy looked sideways in surprise. Spiro had no more to give. He could only watch in horror as Olly raced past him and crossed the finish line first!

But Olly couldn't stop there. Kerberos was right behind him, yapping and barking. His master might have lost the race, but Kerberos wasn't giving up until he'd had a bite out of the new champion!

While the crowd cheered and whistled, Olly circled round the track towards Chloe. Kerberos snarled and snapped in his wake.

Chloe danced up and down. "I knew you could beat Spiro!" she cheered.

"Thanks!" Olly shouted back. "Now, can you get this stupid dog under control?"

"Well done, son, I'm so proud of you," Ariston said, nudging Olly towards the podium to be awarded his prize as the new running champion.

Olly bent his head to receive the crown of twisted olive leaves. It didn't look like much, but there was no other prize like it.

It was the proudest moment of Olly's life. He had beaten Spiro fair and square – even if Kerberos had helped a little bit!

Olly turned to accept the crowd's applause.

Spiro watched from the shadows, a grim scowl on his face. Kerberos bared his teeth in a menacing grin.

The mean pair didn't worry Olly any more. He was the champion!

Olly turned his gaze to the heavens. "Thank you, Hermes," he whispered. "Thank you for your help when I needed it most."

But deep down, Olly knew that he had won the race all by himself.

OLYMPIC FACTS!

DID YOU KNOW...?

The ancient Olympic Games began over 2,700 years ago in Olympia, in southwest Greece.

The ancient Games were were held in honour of Zeus, king of the gods, and were staged every four years at Olympia.

Athletes in the ancient Games usually competed absolutely stark naked!

Running races were held in the *Stadion*, which was about 192 metres long. The course was said to have been paced out by the Greek hero, Herakles.

The ancient Olympics inspired the modern Olympic Games, which began in 1896 in Athens, Greece. Today, the modern Olympic Games are still held every four years in a different city around the world.

OLYMPIA

SHOO RAYNER

All priced at £4.99

Orchard Books are available from all good bookshops, or can be ordered from our website, www.orchardbooks.co.uk, or telephone 01235 827702, or fax 01235 827703.